A
Home for
Sandy

A Home for Sandy

by Holly Webb
Illustrated by Sophy Williams

tiger tales

tiger tales

5 River Road, Suite 128, Wilton, CT 06897
Published in the United States 2017
Originally published in Great Britain 2015
as *A Home for Molly* by the Little Tiger Group
Text copyright © 2015 Holly Webb
Illustrations copyright © 2015 Sophy Williams
Author photograph copyright © Nigel Bird
ISBN-13: 978-1-68010-408-0
ISBN-10: 1-68010-408-X
Printed in China
STP/1800/0126/0317
All rights reserved
10 9 8 7 6 5 4 3 2 1

For more insight and activities, visit us at www.tigertalesbooks.com

Contents

For Mia

Chapter One
Vacation Time

Anna lay on her front in the sand, trying to build a tower of pebbles. It was tricky because she was holding a cheese sandwich, so she only had one hand free for building. She really didn't have room for another sandwich, but since they were on vacation, her mom had let her put ketchup on them, so she didn't want to waste it.

"Anna, did you want a drink?" Mom called over from the picnic blanket. "And some cake?"

"In a minute," Anna said, balancing a large black stone on top of her tower and looking at it hopefully. It wobbled for a second or two—and then the entire thing collapsed. Anna sighed, but she didn't mind that much. It was the fifth time she'd built it and it always fell down in the end. This tower had been higher than any of the others. She got up and wandered back over to the picnic blanket, where her mom and dad were trying to persuade her little sister, Jeannie, that she was too young for cake. Jeannie was only nine months old, but she was convinced that everybody else's food was nicer than hers. Anna thought

she was probably right—some of the
meals in the baby recipe book sounded
very odd. Who would want to eat Tasty
Lentil Surprise?

Anna took her drink and a slice of
cake and moved over to the edge of the
blanket so that Jeannie couldn't see her.
Otherwise it would just be mean.

The beach was really busy today. Anna looked around at all the other families, who were mostly eating their picnics, too. Anna's family had only come to the beach for a quick visit the day before, when they'd first arrived in Seabright. There had been unpacking to do, and Jeannie had been tired after the long car ride. This was their first official beach day. Anna hadn't felt lonely yesterday— it hadn't been the real start of their vacation. But today.... She couldn't help wishing that she had someone else to build sand castles with—or make mermaid statues, like those three girls over by the steps. Or even swim—there was a whole big family group standing by the edge of the water now, the children squealing at the coldness of the waves washing over their toes.

"Oh, *look...*," Anna whispered, as the family's dog splashed through the water, too. She darted into the waves and then shook herself all over the children, making them squeal.

"They're so lucky," Anna said to herself. The dog was beautiful, even when she was wet. Anna wasn't really sure it was a girl dog, of course, but the dog was so pretty—golden-brown and curly all over, with big fluffy ears and blond fur on the top of her head. The seawater had turned her curly fur into coiling tendrils all over. She wasn't very big, and Anna wondered if she was still a puppy.

She watched the family splashing with each other and playing with the dog while she tried to build her tower of stones again. She couldn't help feeling a little jealous. There was an older boy, a girl about her age, and a younger girl as well. They were all laughing and flicking water at each other.

Anna sighed and looked around at Mom and Dad and Jeannie. Her little sister was cute and Anna adored her— most of the time. But it was going to be a while before Jeannie would be big enough to play in the ocean with her.

And the other family had a beautiful fluffy puppy, too! Anna loved dogs, and she really wished they could have one of their own. Dad had said maybe—when Jeannie was bigger. He'd had a dog when he was Anna's age and he loved them, too. But he said he didn't think a dog was a good idea with Jeannie being so tiny—and grabby. Even the nicest dog would get grumpy if Jeannie pulled at its ears, he pointed out, and Anna had to admit that he was right. Jeannie was always pulling her hair and it hurt, even though Jeannie didn't mean it to.

The children were coming out of the water now, heading back to their spot further along the beach by the steps. Anna could see their mom and dad waving. The fluffy little golden dog was racing along the beach after them, stopping to sniff here and there. Anna giggled as she saw the puppy gobble down a bit of sandwich that someone had dropped, and then sniff at a pile of seaweed. She looked like she might be about to eat that, too, and Anna wondered if she should tell the children. Seaweed wasn't the kind of thing that would be good for a dog to eat. Anna frowned disapprovingly as they hurried back to their parents along the beach. How could they not notice that their dog had been about to eat something disgusting? She couldn't help thinking that if *she* had such a perfect dog, she would take better care of it than that.

But then the golden puppy stopped nibbling at the seaweed and raced after the children, flinging herself at their legs and yapping. The older girl was just walking past Anna and her tower of stones, and the little dog was so excited that she knocked it over with her wagging tail.

"Oh! I'm really sorry!" the girl said, looking down in horror at the pile. "I didn't mean to knock it over."

"It's okay! It was an accident. The dog knocked it over with her tail," Anna said, a little shyly. "She's beautiful."

"She is, isn't she?" the other girl agreed, watching as the puppy ran off after her little sister. "Her name is Sandy. Do you want me to help you build your tower again? I was looking at it as we came past—it was really tall! I bet I couldn't do that, but I could pass you the stones or something."

Anna smiled at her. "Don't worry. I was only building it because I was bored. It falls down every time. I must have built about 17 towers by now."

"You're bored?" The girl looked

surprised. She glanced around the beach, as though she couldn't see how anyone could be bored in such a nice place.

"My dad says he'll come in the ocean with me later," Anna explained. "But right now he's watching my baby sister and giving my mom a break. And he says it's not a good idea to go in the ocean on my own. I suppose I could paddle, but…." She shrugged. "You're so lucky having your brother and sister to play with."

The other girl sat down next to Anna and let out a huffy sigh. "You think? Didn't you see Zach push me into that wave? Having a big brother is *awful.*" She sniffed. "Little sisters are a bit better, but Lily always wants to do everything I'm doing, which is a real pain sometimes." She grinned at Anna and nodded over at Jeannie. "You'll find out! But I guess I am lucky, really. It wouldn't be as much fun here without them to do things with." She glanced back at Anna. "You could come and build sand castles with us, if you like. My mom says the tide's going to be high in an hour, so if we want to get the water to go around the castle, now's the time to build it. Would your mom and dad let you?"

Anna nodded. "I'm sure they would. I'll ask. Um, thanks," she added, turning red. "That's really nice of you."

"I'm Rachel," the girl said, jumping up. "I'll come with you. Then I can show your mom and dad where all our stuff is. We were going to build our castle just over there."

Anna's mom was delighted that she'd found someone to play with.

"Of course you can," she said, smiling at Rachel. "It's very kind of you to let Anna join in. Are you the same age as Anna? Nine?"

"I'm almost 10," Rachel said. "And my brother Zach is 12 and Lily is seven. They're both over there." She pointed across the beach. "Oh, they've started. We'd better go, or Zach will build it all wrong."

Anna picked up her shovel and followed Rachel over to her brother and sister. Zach was already digging enthusiastically, making a channel for the water to flow into the moat, and Lily was collecting stones and seashells to decorate the castle. Sandy was helping her, sniffing at the piles of seaweed again and digging shells out for her to pick up.

Anna and Rachel started to build the main part of the castle, digging out a deep moat and piling the sand into the middle to make the fort. Every so often they had to stop and shoo away Lily, who kept trying to stand on the mound of sand.

"I'm bigger than you!" she sang to Rachel.

Rachel rolled her eyes. "Yes, Lily, *because you're standing on a big pile of sand!*"

Anna giggled and Rachel shrugged at her. "Just you wait," she muttered, elbowing Anna in a friendly sort of way. "Oh, look, look! The water's starting to come in!"

A creamy yellow foam was creeping slowly down Zach's channel, and the girls danced up and down excitedly, waiting for it to get right into the moat.

"This wave! It's going to be this one!" Anna yelped. "Look! There it is! Oh, no…."

Sandy had been watching the water suspiciously, glaring at it as it inched along. Now she leaped into the moat and stood there barking at it, sand showering down from the castle all over her golden coat.

"You're going to need a bath tonight," Anna giggled. "Come on! Come on!" She coaxed the little dog out and sat down next to her, patting her gently as they watched the water spread all around the moat. Rachel crouched next to them and petted Sandy's ears.

"Look, it's meeting in the middle!"

Rachel squealed, jumping up and almost falling in the moat herself before sitting back down again.

Anna gave the surprised puppy a hug and then laughed as Sandy licked her nose. "I'm so glad you knocked down my tower," she whispered in Sandy's curly ear.

Chapter Two
Playtime on the Beach

Sandy lay on the sand between Anna and Rachel, her eyes half-closed. One of the girls was scratching her behind the ears, just where she was itchy, and the sun was warm on her back. She could feel that she needed brushing, to get the sand and salt out of her coat, but she was warm and comfortable so she didn't mind.

"Want to play baseball?"

Sandy twitched her ears and looked up as the girls began to talk over her head. The boy was standing there with a ball, so she jumped up with an excited little woof.

"Oh, she wants to play!" Anna laughed. "Do you like chasing balls, Sandy?"

"As long as she doesn't eat the ball," Zach said doubtfully. "Still, I suppose she can get it if Lily hits it into the water!"

"I won't!" Lily yelled, stamping her foot, and Sandy edged back, looking worried.

"Oh, she's scared. Be careful, Lily; you frightened her, shouting like that. Good dog, Sandy." Rachel crouched down and petted her, and Sandy licked her hand gratefully. She didn't like it when people were loud. But she soon forgot that she'd been scared as she raced around for the ball, barking excitedly as the children laughed and chased after her.

"She's the best fielder I've ever seen," Zach said, grinning. "Come on, Sandy. Give me the ball! Come on—oh, no, Sandy! I could have gotten Rachel out if you hadn't held on to it."

"She's on our side," Rachel said smugly. "Good dog, Sandy. Oh, look, Mom has cookies. I'll give you one when she's not looking."

Sandy wagged her tail blissfully and wolfed down the sweet cookie, looking hopefully over to the girls for more.

Anna giggled. "Oh, go ahead. You can have half of mine—I'm not that hungry. I suppose you're growing, and you need the energy!"

Sandy gobbled the cookie and flopped down on Anna's feet, sleepy after all the racing around that she'd done. She was still hungry, of course, but the cookies had been very, very good.

It was one of the best afternoons that Anna had had in a long time. But all too soon, Rachel's mom and dad were rolling up their towels and sending everyone to find the shovels and boogie boards and balls that they'd left scattered all over the sand.

"Will you be at the beach tomorrow?" Rachel asked hopefully, and Anna nodded. She'd wanted to ask the same thing, but what if Rachel didn't want her hanging around with them again?

"Oh, Rachel, I think we might be going to that amusement park tomorrow," her mom said, looking up from putting away all the damp things. "We're not quite sure. But maybe we'll see you the day after, Anna."

Anna nodded and smiled, then wandered back to Mom, Dad, and Jeannie.

"They were so friendly," her mom said, smiling. She'd chatted with Rachel's mom and dad for a bit when she'd come over to check on Anna.

"They probably aren't coming to the beach tomorrow, though," Anna sighed, flumping down onto the sand next to Mom.

"Well, I owe you a swim. We'll definitely do that tomorrow," Dad pointed out. "It's getting chilly now that the wind's picking up. Might be time to think about going back to the beach house. Don't worry, Anna. I promise you'll have fun tomorrow. I'll take you in the ocean, and we could bring the kite down, too."

Anna smiled at him. Dad was right— she would love going in the water to swim. It was just that everything seemed quiet and flat now without Rachel and the others.

"I just thought of something," Dad said, looking worried.

"What?" Anna asked anxiously— Dad was really frowning.

"We've been on the beach for an entire day, and none of us has had ice cream!"

"Oh, Dad! I thought something terrible had happened!" Anna grinned.

"That *is* terrible! Come on. Help me fold up the picnic blanket, and we'll go to the ice-cream shop on the way back."

Sandy watched as the children trailed away along the path up to the top of the cliff, carrying bags and pails and sandy shoes. They had played with her and petted her all afternoon, and for the first time in a long time, she had felt as though she had really belonged to someone. But now they were leaving, and she was left behind again.

She had tried to follow them, but the older girl had shooed her back. "Go on, Sandy! Go home! Go and find your owners—that's them over there, isn't it?

Those boys?"

Sandy gave a hopeful whimper and tried again, trotting along behind them, but the man had pushed her gently back toward the beach and told her no. She knew they wouldn't let her stay, even if she did sneak after them again.

So she went back to the beach and sat by the little stand that sold the ice cream and beach toys. They had a bowl of water outside for dogs, and she was thirsty after running around in the sun all afternoon. The stand sold hot dogs and sandwiches, too, and she'd found leftovers in their garbage cans before. But she couldn't go digging through the cans until later on, or the owner would shout at her and chase her away.

"That's such a cute little dog," a girl said as she came away from the stand carrying an ice-cream cone. "I wonder who she belongs to."

The girl's mother looked over at Sandy and smiled. "Oh, she's with that family sitting down by the steps. I saw them playing with her. She is sweet, isn't she?"

The beach was emptying out now, just a few people left and all of those slowly packing up their things. Sandy watched them hopefully, wondering if there would be any scraps left when they were gone.

The lady who ran the ice-cream stand came out to fold up her shutters, and Sandy skittered away behind one of the other stands before the lady could shout at her. She scurried along behind the line of stands and came out by the steps. She would go and sniff along the line of broken shells and seaweed down by the water. She'd found things to eat mixed up in there before.

Sandy dragged her paws over the deep sand, feeling weary. She had loved playing with the children that afternoon, but now she was worn out and so hungry. The seaweed smelled strong and salty, and there was another smell—a hopeful sort of smell. A fish! She scratched at it excitedly with her paw, and it broke into pieces.

Sandy sneezed at the smell—it had been dead for a while and didn't smell very nice. It was dry and leathery from lying there all afternoon in the hot sun. She could just about remember the delicious pieces of fish she used to get as a treat when she'd lived with her owners, before she was a stray—this fish smelled very different. But Sandy was too hungry to be picky. She wolfed it down, even the bones and the dried-up skin.

After the fish, Sandy padded along the sand to the little hollow under the patch of tall grass. This was the wilder end of the beach, past the concrete sidewalk, where the road led down to the harbor. It was never as busy, so there wasn't as much chance of scraps from a picnic. But the dunes were a quiet place to sleep. Sandy had found a sandy hole under a big clump of grass a few weeks before. She'd then dug it out a little more, so that it made a nest just large enough for a small dog to sleep under cover. She snuggled into it and curled up. Her stomach was hurting—the fish probably hadn't been a good thing to eat. But it had been all there was.

Chapter Three
The Lost Dog

The next day, Anna and her parents packed the picnic things under Jeannie's stroller again and got ready to set off for the beach. Anna had been hopping around by the front door for what seemed like forever. When they'd stopped at the ice-cream shop the day before, she had spotted a boogie board with dolphins on it, and she'd been admiring it while the lady behind the counter scooped their ice cream. The dolphins were beautiful—they looked as though they were smiling, and Anna couldn't help smiling back at them. Then she'd heard Dad saying, "And we'll take that boogie board, too, please."

Anna had wheeled around, staring at him in surprise. She hadn't even asked, just thought how much fun it would be to have one. A lot of people on the beach that day had been splashing around on them.

Now, she was desperate to get down there and try it out. It just seemed to be taking forever for Mom and Dad to finish laying out the picnic and Jeannie's things. Anna had run around finding all of her sister's toys, but now Jeannie needed her diaper changed.

Eventually, Dad lifted the stroller over the front step and they set off along the clifftop path to the beach.

"Looking forward to trying out your boogie board?" he asked, watching Anna admire the dolphins again as she carried it along.

"It's going to be great," Anna told him, as she tried to squash down the thought that it would be even more fun with a friend. Still, she had Dad to swim with, which was going to be fun, too. He often worked really late, so Anna didn't see him that much except on weekends and during the holidays.

As soon as Dad had helped spread out the picnic blanket and unload all their picnic stuff, he and Anna picked their way over the pebbles and sand down to the ocean. It was a beautiful hot day, and the water was calm.

"The water is really blue today," Anna said, sounding surprised. "Yesterday it was sort of brownish-green."

"Maybe it's reflecting the sky," Dad suggested. "Are you ready for this, Anna?" He grinned at her. "You don't want to back out?"

"No!" Anna glared at him. "Although it does look a little cold," she admitted.

Dad tested the water with one foot. "Ugh. Make that very cold."

"Go on!" Mom called. She was standing further up the beach next to Jeannie, holding up her phone to take a picture. "It'll be nice and warm when you get in."

Dad sighed. "That's because we'll be so numb with cold we won't be able to feel it! Come on, Anna—let's run." He grabbed Anna's hand and they dashed into the water. It *was* cold. Freezing. But Mom was right. After a couple of minutes, it really didn't feel cold at all.

They had the best morning splashing around with the boogie board, Dad swimming along, towing Anna behind him, and jumping in and out of the waves. Then Dad helped Anna build a sand castle that was even bigger than the one she and Rachel and the others had made the day before.

After lunch, Jeannie was fussy and cranky, so Mom and Dad took turns playing with her and carrying her up and down the beach, trying to convince her she wanted a nap. She didn't, though. She kept on crying, and Anna knew there was no use asking Dad if he wanted to go in the water again. She lay on her front on the sun-warmed pebbles, reading her book.

By about three o'clock, Mom was starting to look really anxious. Even Anna was feeling worried—her little sister looked so miserable. "Mom, should we go back to the beach house?" she suggested, looking at Jeannie's scarlet cheeks. "Maybe Jeannie just doesn't want to sleep in her stroller. If we went back, you could put her down in the play yard, and she might feel better."

"Would you mind?" Mom asked,

looking at Anna gratefully. "I don't want to spoil your beach day, Anna. We only have a week here. Maybe Dad could stay with you and I'll take Jeannie back."

"I'd rather come with you," Anna said, with one quick wistful glance at the ocean. "I've got that bead jewelry kit that Nana bought me for Christmas, and I'd like to do some of that. And anyway, I think it's going to rain." She didn't really—there was only one tiny cloud in the sky—but she wanted to make Mom feel better.

They started to pack up, folding the towels and gathering all their things together. As they were walking along the sidewalk to the cliff path, Anna stopped for a last look at the ocean. *It'll still be there tomorrow,* she told herself.

And I bet Jeannie will feel better by then. Maybe Mom will go in the water with me. Rachel might be back on the beach, too. She was just about to turn around and run after her mom and dad when she saw a dog—a little golden, curly-haired dog, trotting along the sidewalk a short way behind her.

"That looks just like Sandy," Anna muttered to herself, squinting thoughtfully at the little dog. "But it can't be. I haven't seen Rachel and the others. And I did look all the way down the beach when we got here."

"Anna! Come on!" Dad called, waving to her.

Anna turned to wave back. "Coming!" she answered. But then she looked at the dog again. She was almost certain it was Sandy—the dark eyes were just the same, and the messy curls around her muzzle and ears. "It *is* her! Sandy, what are you doing here on your own?" Even if she *had* just missed Rachel's family and they were here after all, Sandy was too far away from them now. Had she run off?

47

"They should keep you on a leash," Anna said worriedly. She glanced over at Dad, who was starting to look a little angry. She'd have to go and explain. Anna dashed along the sidewalk to where he was waiting at the bottom of the path. Mom had already set off with the stroller.

"Come on, sweetheart. We really need to get home. Mom thinks Jeannie has a tooth coming through."

"Dad, can we stop? I just saw Sandy— you know, Rachel's dog? She's back there and Rachel's not here. I think Sandy's lost."

Dad glanced worriedly up the path. "Are you sure, Anna? This isn't a good time to stop...."

"I know! But I'm really worried.

What if something happens to her? If she goes up the path she could end up on the road."

Dad sighed. "All right. You go and see if you can get her to come to you. I'll text your mom and tell her what's happening."

Anna dropped her bag of swimming things and raced back through the people wandering along the sidewalk.

"Sandy! Sandy!" she cried, looking around for the golden puppy. "She was just here," she said. "I'm sure she was." But there was no little dog to be seen, and Sandy didn't come when Anna called.

"Did you find her?" Dad asked, catching up with Anna.

"No!" she said anxiously. "And I'm

sure it was Sandy, Dad, I really am. What will I say to Rachel, Zach, and Lily? I should have gone after her right away."

"They're probably further down the beach somewhere and she's gone back to them," Dad said soothingly. "Don't panic, Anna."

"But they're *not* here," Anna explained, trying not to let her voice wobble. "I've looked. And their mom said they were probably going to an amusement park today. They must have left Sandy behind at their beach house, and she slipped out somehow. I don't know what to do!"

"Well, at the moment, there isn't anything we can do. Besides, you might just have mistaken another dog for Sandy. There are a lot of dogs on the beach—it's one of the nice things about Seabright. I mean, look. That little spaniel over there looks a lot like the dog you were playing with yesterday."

Anna looked over eagerly to where Dad was pointing, hoping that he'd spotted Sandy. But it wasn't—the spaniel was cute and curly-eared, but it had much darker fur than the golden-haired puppy, and it wasn't all frizzy and curly.

"She's just disappeared," Anna said sadly. "Oh, Sandy, where are you?"

Chapter Four
Searching for Sandy

Sandy padded along the seafront, sniffing for food. A little boy had given her half a sandwich at lunchtime, but then his mom had scolded him and shooed her away. Half a sandwich was not enough to fill her up, and now she felt empty and miserable.

There was a delicious smell coming from somewhere up ahead—so good that Sandy couldn't stop her tail from wagging with delight. She hurried along, sniffing hopefully and trying to figure out where the food was.

A family was sitting outside one of the café stands, eating their fried fish dinners. It smelled so good that Sandy felt herself begin to drool a little. She crept closer, her tail moving from side to side in a shy wag. She sat down next to a girl who was sitting in a canvas chair and looked up at her. She glanced between the girl and the fries, her dark brown eyes pleading. *Can I have some, please?*

The girl giggled, peeked over at her mom and dad to check that they weren't looking, and sneaked Sandy a fry.

"You're so cute," she whispered. "I bet you're not allowed to have these, though. Where's your owner? Did you get off your leash?" she added, giving Sandy another fry.

"Is that a dog, Ella?" her mom called over.

"Yes, look. Isn't she pretty?"

"I hope you're not feeding her!"

"Oh, no, of course not." Ella grinned down at Sandy. "Our secret," she whispered. "But they'll see if I give you any more, sorry."

Suddenly, there was a wild flurry of barking, and a big golden Labrador surged out from under one of the chairs, almost knocking over the man who was sitting in it. He yelled loudly, and Sandy backed away, turning tail and running as the huge Labrador raced after her. He was much bigger than she was, and his legs were a lot longer, too. Even though he'd gotten caught up in all the chairs, he was soon right on her tail, barking and growling furiously. She had been bothering his people.

Sandy raced along the sidewalk as fast as she could, but she didn't have very much energy—not like the Labrador, who was fit and well-fed. He caught her, knocking her down with one of his massive paws and rolling her on the concrete. He stood over her, growling and showing his massive teeth, and Sandy whimpered with fear, her paws in the air, trying to show that she wouldn't fight. She was sorry—he was in charge.

"Hugo! Get off!" The man who'd

almost been knocked over and the nice girl came racing up.

"Get off that poor little dog!" the girl shrieked.

"Bad dog, Hugo!" The man grabbed Hugo's collar and dragged him away from Sandy.

"Awww, she's so scared, poor little thing," the girl said, crouching down by Sandy. "Where's your owner? We'd better go and take you back, and apologize for Hugo chasing you."

"I'm not sure she has an owner," the man said, still trying to hold Hugo back. The big dog was growling and trying to lunge at Sandy. "Hugo, stop it! No!" he said firmly, and Hugo edged away, still growling. "I think I saw her the other day by the ice-cream stand. Maybe she's a stray? But she's such a nice little dog. I'd be surprised if people weren't looking for her."

Sandy peered sideways at the big Labrador and realized that he wasn't about to chase her again. She sprang up, trembling, and backed away, step by step.

"Oh, no, come back!" the girl cried. "We need to find out who you belong to!"

But Sandy was already gone. As soon 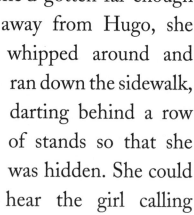 as she'd gotten far enough away from Hugo, she whipped around and ran down the sidewalk, darting behind a row of stands so that she was hidden. She could hear the girl calling behind her, but that big dog was there, too. She couldn't go back.

Anna sat at the kitchen table with her bead kit, listening to Jeannie fussing upstairs and worrying about the puppy.

"Oh, no," she muttered, looking at the bracelet she was threading. She'd done it wrong again—for about the third time. She just couldn't concentrate. Anna was sure it had been Sandy she'd seen on the beach. She kept wondering if the little dog had gotten home yet.

59

Maybe Rachel and her family were out looking for her—if only she could go and tell them where she'd last seen Sandy, it might help. But she didn't even know where Rachel's beach house was.

Anna stood up and went over to the window. At least it was still light out. The only time that she remembered being lost herself was a few years before, when she had been Christmas shopping with Mom. She had stopped to look at a beautiful window display, with a toy Santa Claus that waved. She had been transfixed—and then she'd turned around to point out Santa Claus, and her mom was gone.

It had been late afternoon and getting dark—just the right time to see all the sparkling Christmas lights, but

60

the darkness had made Anna feel even more scared.

Mom had found her, of course. She had only gone a few steps up the street before she realized that Anna wasn't right beside her anymore. She'd come dashing back and scooped up Anna and hugged her. But Anna still remembered that panicked moment in the dark when she thought that she was lost forever. Now she wondered if Sandy was feeling the same way. She turned around from the window and marched determinedly up the stairs. Mom and Dad were trying to give Jeannie some medicine to help with the teething, but she kept spitting it out.

"Oh, hello, sweetie." Mom looked up at her worriedly. "Are you all right,

Anna? Do you want to grab an apple, or some cheese, or something? I'm really sorry—we haven't even started making dinner yet. It's going to be a while."

"It's okay, Mom. I'm not hungry. I was just wondering if I could walk down to the beach and look at the ocean. I won't be long—it's this beautiful blue color right now, and I want to see it closer."

Their beach house went straight out onto the path along the top of the cliff, so there were no roads to cross. Anna crossed her fingers hopefully behind her back. She hated lying to Mom and Dad, but she wasn't really lying, she told herself. The ocean *was* that beautiful color, and she would look at it—it was just that she would be looking for a little curly-haired dog *more*. If she'd said that she was going out to search for Sandy, she was pretty sure Dad would say no—he hadn't been very happy when she'd made him spend a long time looking for her earlier.

"I'll be back by the time dinner is ready—or I could come back and help make it. Do you want me to turn the oven on or anything?" Anna suggested.

Dad sighed. "At this rate we'll be heading out to get fried fish dinners, Anna. Don't worry. Be back soon, all right? And no talking to strangers."

"I promise." Anna dashed into her room to grab a sweater and raced back downstairs and out the door before they could change their minds.

Chapter Five
Finding Sandy's Home

"Sandy! Sandy!"

Sandy was curled up under the ice-cream stand, where she'd run after the huge Labrador had chased her. She had been so frightened that she felt shaky and for a long time, she couldn't stop panting. Her tail was still tucked tightly between her legs, and she had curled herself into the smallest ball she could, right at the back of the stand where it stood against the cliff wall. Exhausted, she'd fallen into an uneasy sleep, twitching as the big dog ran after her in her dreams.

She woke up with a start, feeling puzzled. Was someone calling her? She was almost sure she'd heard her name. Her ears pricked up—as much as her frizzy, curly ears ever did—and she listened intently. But there was no one there. Sandy sighed and turned around a few times on the dusty, sandy concrete, trying to go back to sleep. She would wait a while longer before she trotted down to her comfy hollow in the long grass. She wanted to make sure that the Labrador really was gone.

Sandy laid her nose down on her paws and tried to ignore how hungry she felt—a few fries didn't go far. She was just starting to snooze when she heard the voice again. She was sure this time. Someone *was* calling her name!

Sandy wriggled forward under the stand until she could see out from behind the little steps at the front.

Standing on the sidewalk was a girl—the girl she had played with on the beach, who had given her a cookie!

"Sandy! Sandy! Please come out!"

Sandy yelped and scratched her way

from behind the steps, darting across the sidewalk to Anna.

"Sandy! You're here! Oh, it really is you! I was right." Anna rubbed the excited little dog's ears and laughed as Sandy danced around her. "Oh, Sandy, you're so messy! You're all covered in sand and dirt. I'm so glad I found you—I thought maybe I'd imagined it and it hadn't been you that I saw at all." Then she stopped and frowned. "It's great that I found you, Sandy. But we've still got to get you home, and I don't know where Rachel and the others are staying." Anna sat down on the edge of the sidewalk with her feet in the sand and her arm around Sandy.

Sandy licked Anna's face, delighted that she could reach it now.

"Ughhh, Sandy!" Anna rubbed it off and gave the puppy a hug. "All Rachel said was that your house was really close to the ice-cream shop—the same one where I got my boogie board. She said it was great, because they were always going past it and if they all begged, her mom almost always said yes…. So I guess we'll just have to go and look around there. Maybe we'll see Rachel or Lily or Zach looking out of a window or something." She gazed down at Sandy doubtfully. "I wish I had a leash for you, sweetheart. I don't really want to take you across the road without holding onto you properly." She shuddered at the thought of Sandy dashing out in front of a car. "Mom and Dad make a big enough deal about *me* crossing roads, even if they do let me walk most of the way home from school now." She looked around, hoping for a piece of string or something that she could tie through Sandy's worn collar.

"Oh! Your collar! Maybe you have Rachel's mom or dad's number on there. Let's hope it's a cell phone…." She turned the collar around carefully, looking for the tag. Sandy's fur was matted underneath it, and Anna bit her lip. She really liked Rachel's family, but she didn't think they were taking very good care of Sandy. The poor little dog needed a really good brushing—probably a trim from a dog groomer, too. "No tag…. It just has 'Sandy' woven on as part of the collar. That's no good. Oh, well, maybe the tag with the number came off." Anna sighed. "Back to Plan A, then." She was just looking at a heap of seaweed and wondering if she could twist it together to make a rope when she rolled her eyes. "I'm so silly, Sandy. My scarf!"

Anna was wearing a pretty flowered bandanna that Mom had bought her to wear over her hair instead of a sunhat. She pulled it off and untied the knot, stretching it out. It wasn't very long, but it would be okay if she bent down a little.

"Here, Sandy. A nice new leash. Look." She tied one corner of the bandanna through the strong metal ring on Sandy's collar and stood up, keeping a tight hold of the other end. "That'll do…. Come on, Sandy! Let's take you home!"

Sandy walked along beside Anna as they headed up the path steps to the top of the cliff. She sniffed happily at the clumps of wild plants that were growing out over the concrete steps, and Anna smiled down at her proudly. She was so beautiful, even if she was a little scruffy. As they walked along the seafront path, Anna couldn't help pretending that Sandy was her dog. She could imagine it for five minutes, couldn't she?

But the walk to the ice-cream shop was much too short. Soon Anna was standing outside and staring at the closed shutters. If it had still been open, she could have stopped by to ask if they happened to know where Rachel's family was staying, since Rachel figured that they were the shop's best customers.

"There are a lot of houses along here, Sandy," Anna said, looking around at the lawn surrounded by beach houses. "I suppose I'm just going to have to ring the doorbells and ask." But she stood on the grassy patch for a little while, hoping she'd suddenly see Rachel. She hated the thought of having to ask at all those houses. She'd told Mom and Dad she wouldn't talk to strangers, for a start. And what if Rachel's family wasn't even staying in one of them? Maybe they were on one of the streets close to the lawn.

Anna sighed. She was just going to have to be brave. She marched over to the closest house and rang the bell. There were pails and shovels in the doorway, so at least there were children here.

The door opened, and Anna found herself staring at a boy a little older than herself—but it definitely wasn't Zach. And there was a smaller boy peering around him, too.

"Oh! Sorry! Wrong house," Anna stammered. "Um, you don't happen to know where Zach and Rachel are staying, do you?"

"No," the boy said, staring at her as though she were crazy.

"Sorry...." Anna backed away, blushing scarlet and gently tugging Sandy after her.

"I should have explained why I was asking," Anna muttered to Sandy, as they went on to the next house. "Oh, that was so embarrassing."

No one answered at the following

two houses—which Anna was secretly relieved about. The next door was opened by a friendly-looking lady, who smiled at Sandy and said, "Oh, what a sweet dog."

"She isn't mine," Anna said, grateful that the lady had made it easy for her to explain. "I found her on the beach, but I know who she belongs to, and I'm pretty sure they're staying around here. They told me they were in a house by the ice-cream shop. No one has asked about a dog, have they? There are three children—a boy and two girls."

The lady looked at the houses around the lawn thoughtfully. "It's very nice of you to try to bring her home. I wonder if it's Mrs. Merritt's family. I know they were staying with her, and she does have three grandchildren. She told me she was going to have trouble squeezing them and their dog all in, especially now that her grandson is so tall."

"Oh!" Anna said delightedly. "That sounds right! Zach is really tall. Where does she live?"

"That white house over there on the corner. Good luck! If you don't find her owners, do you know where the vet is? I'm sure they'd help you out—it's just around the corner from here."

"Thanks!" Anna beamed at her. "Come on, Sandy." She patted her leg and Sandy scampered after her across the grass to the white house. Anna hurried up the little path between the bright flowerbeds and rang the doorbell firmly, not feeling as nervous as she had before. She was sure this had to be the right place, even though Rachel hadn't mentioned that they were staying with their grandma.

It took a long time for someone to anwer the door, though. Wasn't that a bit strange? Wouldn't Rachel or Zach or Lily have run to get it? Maybe they were out. In fact, they were probably out looking for Sandy. Anna sighed and pressed the bell one last time, just in case.

The door swung open sharply and a very angry-looking elderly lady stared at Anna.

"What is it? Couldn't you tell that I was coming? I was asleep—so rude!"

"Oh…. Oh, I'm really sorry." Anna backed away and so did Sandy, with a little whimper. "The lady across the street thought this might be your grandchildren's dog—she said they were staying with you."

"Of course it isn't. They have a Jack Russell. And they went home yesterday."

"I'm really sorry. I didn't mean to wake you up. I was just trying to find the dog's owners, that's all." Anna swallowed, trying not to cry. The elderly lady seemed so grumpy.

"Hmm. Well, I hope you find them." The lady looked slightly less annoyed. "There are children in the house two houses down that way—why don't you try there?"

Anna nodded. "Thank you," she said, hurrying off as fast as she could and ringing the bell at the house that the lady had pointed to.

She had to stand on the step for a few moments, but when the door opened, it was worth the wait. "Oh, thank goodness it's you!" she gasped, as Rachel peered around the door in front of her.

Chapter Six
The Truth About Sandy

"Did you come to visit? It's Anna," Rachel called back into the house. "My friend from the beach, Mom." Rachel smiled at Anna and then looked down at Sandy. "Oh! You brought Sandy, too."

She looked a little bit puzzled, Anna thought. "Hadn't you noticed she was gone?" she asked Rachel. Sandy had been out since the middle of the afternoon! It seemed strange that they hadn't noticed.

Rachel frowned. "Gone where?"

"She was running along the beach this afternoon, but I couldn't catch her," Anna explained. "I told Mom and Dad I was going to see the ocean, so I could look for her again. She must have slipped out earlier—or maybe you left her on the beach," she added doubtfully. She couldn't imagine being that careless, but Rachel didn't seem to have a clue where her dog was....

"We haven't been to the beach," Rachel said slowly. "We went to an amusement park. We just got back a little while ago."

Anna nodded. "She slipped out, then." She crouched down and rubbed Sandy's poor scruffy ears that needed brushing so badly. She was almost tempted not to give Sandy back....

Rachel crouched down, too, and Sandy sniffed her fingers in a friendly sort of way. Anna watched, frowning a little. Sandy didn't seem that excited to see her owner.

"Anna, I don't understand." Rachel looked at her over Sandy's head. "Why would we notice Sandy was gone? And gone *where*?"

"Don't you care about her at all?" Anna felt her eyes filling with tears. How could Rachel not even be worried that Sandy had been out on her own all day? She could have been run over! "She's your dog! You're supposed to take care of her!"

Rachel simply stared at her for a moment. Then she shook her head. "No, she isn't," she said slowly.

"What?"

"She's not our dog, Anna." Rachel frowned. "She doesn't belong to us. We don't even *have* a dog."

"But she was with you on the beach!"

Anna looked down at Sandy, who was watching them anxiously.

The little dog wagged her tail, very faintly. She could tell they were getting angry with each other, Anna realized, and she patted Sandy's ears gently. "It's okay," she said. Then she looked up at Rachel. "She's really not yours? I was so sure…. She was with us all that afternoon. And you knew her name—you told me she was named Sandy!"

"Yes, because it's on her collar." Rachel pointed to the name, woven into the fabric. "She was watching us playing in the water, and then she just tagged along. She was so beautiful—but I thought she belonged to those teenage boys who were sitting further up the beach. I was sure she did." Rachel frowned. "I thought they were mean, not playing with her…. And they didn't seem to mind her being with us, so I just kept paying attention to her."

"Oh, wow," Anna muttered. "I guess I just thought she was yours because of the way you apologized about her knocking over my tower. I'm sorry," she added. "I was really being mean just now. You must have thought I was crazy!"

"That's all right," said Rachel. "I would have done the same if I thought you weren't taking care of your dog. But how did you find us? I never told you the address of the beach house, did I? I wished I'd thought of giving you Mom's cell phone number so we could meet up on the beach again. I was so angry with myself last night when I realized I couldn't even call you!"

Anna sighed. "You told me you were staying near the ice-cream shop, so I knocked on doors. It was so embarrassing. And the lady two doors down was really angry with me!"

"Ooooh, she exploded at Lily the other day because she spilled sand out of her pail onto the pavement. I think she's just a bit grumpy. You poor thing." Rachel put her arm around Anna's shoulders and gave her a hug. "I'm sorry you got into trouble."

Anna smiled at her, but then her smile faded. "It doesn't matter—but Rachel, if Sandy doesn't belong to you, then whose dog *is* she?"

"I don't know." Rachel looked worriedly at Sandy. "I thought she belonged to those boys, the same way you thought she was ours. I never actually saw them call her or anything...."

"Do you think she could be a stray and that maybe she doesn't belong to anyone? She's so scruffy. Sorry, Sandy— you're beautiful, but you *are* scruffy," Anna told her. "I mean, she needs grooming really badly, and she's covered in sand."

"She's too thin, too," Rachel pointed out.

Anna ran her hand over Sandy's head,

and Sandy panted at her happily. "So—
do you think she's a stray?"

"Maybe…," Rachel nodded. "It seems
that way, doesn't it?"

"Poor Sandy," Anna whispered. "I
wonder what happened—she's so pretty,
and she's still only a puppy."

"Maybe she got lost when her
owners were here on vacation," Rachel
suggested sadly. "And they went home
without her."

"That's awful…." Anna swallowed.
"What am I going to do? I thought I was
bringing her home, and now it seems as
though she doesn't have a home at all."

"Rachel, are you two all right out
there?" Rachel's mom came out of
the kitchen. "Hello, Anna. That's a
sweet little dog. You had her with you

on the beach, didn't you?"

Rachel and Anna looked at each other and started to laugh. "Mom, Anna thought Sandy was ours. She brought her back! And now we don't know who she belongs to."

"Oh!" Anna looked down at her watch. "I have to get back. I told Mom and Dad I'd only be a few minutes. I was just supposed to be going to look at the ocean."

"They'll be very worried about you," Rachel's mom said in an alarmed voice that made Anna feel much worse. "We'd better take you home right now." She called out that she'd be back soon and closed the front door behind her. Then she hurried the girls and Sandy down the street.

"Where are you staying, Anna?" she asked. "Can you remember the way?"

"Oh, yes. It's one of the beach-front houses, by the ocean. I can go back by myself, honestly."

But Rachel's mom shook her head. "No, it's all right. I want to make sure that you get home safely."

"Mom," Rachel put in suddenly. "If Sandy's a stray, and we think she might be, can we keep her?"

Anna gasped—it was exactly what she had been thinking. If only she had said something first!

But Rachel's mom shook her head firmly. "No, of course not. For starters, the beach house has a no-pets rule. And what would Barney think if we came home and got him out of the boarding kennel and there was a dog in his house? He'd probably walk out!"

Rachel sighed. "I guess so."

Anna took a deep, shaky breath and wrapped her hand more tightly around Sandy's makeshift leash. Until Rachel had spoken, she'd only had the idea in the back of her mind, but how amazing would it be if Sandy could be hers? After all, no one else seemed to want her.... Why shouldn't they keep her?

"Would you like to stay with me?" she whispered to Sandy as she saw their beach house and hurried ahead. "Would you like to be my dog?" She knocked lightly on the front door of the house— the last thing she wanted to do was wake up Jeannie. She needed Mom and Dad in the best mood possible.

The door swung open at once, and Mom grabbed her into a hug. "Anna, where have you been? You said you'd only be a few minutes. I was about to go out looking for you!"

"I'm sorry, Mom...."

"Anna's actually been really resourceful," Rachel's mom put in. "She found this dog *and* she figured out where we'd been staying so she could bring the poor little thing back to us. Only the dog isn't actually ours."

"Is that the dog you were looking for earlier, Anna?" Dad asked, peering over Mom's shoulder.

"Yes, but she doesn't belong to the other family. We don't know who she belongs to at all." Anna crouched down and picked up Sandy, showing her to Mom and Dad. "She's so beautiful. I can't see how anybody would abandon her."

"I'm sorry we can't take care of her ourselves until her owner is found," Rachel's mom explained. "But we had to sign a no-pets agreement for our beach house."

"I think pets are allowed in this one," Dad said slowly. "But we can't have a dog here—what about Jeannie?"

"Sandy's really friendly, Dad," Anna explained. "She wouldn't snap at Jeannie."

"She was very patient with the children on the beach the other day," Rachel's mom agreed.

"Couldn't we just take care of her for a couple of days, Dad?" Anna suggested hopefully. "I could take her to the vet to see if anyone has reported her lost. And put up posters about her."

She didn't say what she was really thinking, which was, *And then if no one knows anything about her, maybe we can just take her home with us....*

Chapter Seven
Caring for Sandy

Sandy was lying on an old picnic blanket that Anna had found in one of the closets in the living room. She was very sleepy, mostly because she was full. It was the strangest feeling, not to be hungry. She couldn't remember the last time she hadn't been desperate for food.

Anna and her dad had gone to the

supermarket to get some dog food on their way to pick up their fried fish dinners. Jeannie had fallen asleep at last, but her tooth was still making her really miserable. Anna had begged Dad to let her buy a comb, too. She wanted to try and get rid of the worst of the tangles from Sandy's coat.

So now Sandy was well fed and a little less sandy and scruffy. There were still a lot of knots in her fur, though, because the comb hadn't been strong enough, and several of its teeth had snapped off.

"I'll buy you a dog-grooming brush when I go to the vet tomorrow," Anna had told Sandy, as she'd hugged her goodnight. Then she gave a tiny sigh. "I know I should hope that the vet knows who you belong to, but I really don't.

I want you to belong to me." She gave Sandy one last pat and went upstairs.

Sandy stared after her, wondering where Anna was going. She stayed on her blanket, but she kept her eyes on the stairs, watching until she fell asleep. She woke again a couple of hours later to find the house dark and quiet. She was all alone downstairs. Sandy lay on the rug for a while, with her head on her paws. She was still sleepy, but she wanted to know where everyone was. Sandy had lived without an owner for months now, and it had felt so good to have Anna making a big deal about her. She had enjoyed having her fur combed, too, even when the comb got caught in all the tangles and pulled. Somebody wanted her. Somebody cared enough about her to clean her up and make her a comfy bed.

Sandy got up and went to sniff at the bottom of the stairs. *They're all up there,* she thought. All of a sudden, Sandy was desperate to see that Anna hadn't disappeared. It had happened before, after all…. People had gone away and left her. Quickly, she padded up the stairs, sniffing for Anna's room. She found it almost right away, poking her nose around the door.

Anna turned over as her bedroom door creaked open and peered sleepily at the puppy. "Hello, Sandy!" she whispered. "Did you come to find me? Aren't you clever! Oh, you're such a good dog."

Sandy scurried over to the bed. Anna leaned down to pat her. "Sandy, come on," she said. "Come on up here, good dog.... That's it!" She giggled delightedly as Sandy scrambled up onto the end of the bed and curled up blissfully by her feet. It was just the way she'd dreamed having a dog would be.

"So they didn't leave a number?" Anna asked the vet's receptionist. She hated it that Sandy's owners didn't seem to have taken very good care of her at all. Even though the receptionist was almost sure that the people she remembered coming in to ask about their lost dog had been talking about Sandy, she said they were in a rush and hadn't left her their phone number. Sandy wasn't microchipped, either.

Secretly, though, Anna couldn't help feeling relieved. If the vet did have a way to contact Sandy's real owners, Anna would have to give her back. And that was getting harder and harder to imagine.

"There's an animal shelter in Long Branch," the receptionist went on, handing Anna a flyer. "I'm afraid we can't take stray dogs here, although I'd love to. She looks like a little treasure."

"She is sweet," Anna's dad agreed. "I wouldn't mind keeping her, but we've got a small baby, so I just don't think it's a good idea." He looked over Anna's shoulder at the flyer. "Mmm. I suppose we'll have to take her there then. I'd better call your mom."

"Can't we wait a little while?" Anna asked, crossing her fingers in the folds of her skirt and doing her best pleading-eyes look at Dad. "We still don't know for sure that Sandy belonged to those people. It could have been another dog. Rachel and I are going to make posters to put up to tell everybody that we've found her."

Dad nodded thoughtfully. "I guess a day or two wouldn't hurt, just as long as your mom agrees," he said. "But after that, she'll have to go to the shelter."

Rachel had brought a sketchpad and a lot of markers with her on vacation, so she and Anna drew posters that afternoon at Anna's beach house. It was a grayish sort of day, not really the best day for playing out on the beach anyway. Then they borrowed Anna's mom's cell phone, just in case of an emergency, and went out to put up the signs on lampposts and on the railings along the waterfront. "After all, she was on the beach," Rachel pointed out. "So it makes sense that her owners might have lost her there. If they're still looking for her, this is a good place to put a sign."

Too good, Anna thought to herself. She almost felt like tearing the posters down again.

"We've got to get back," Rachel said as they finished putting up the last one. "Mom said she'd come and pick me up from your house at three, and it's five to three now. Oh, do you want to come on a picnic with us tomorrow afternoon? She said it was okay to ask you and your mom and dad, and Jeannie and Sandy, too."

"Yes, please!" Anna nodded eagerly. "But if we're going on a picnic, then we can't take Sandy to the shelter. Dad did say we could keep her for a day or two, though...."

Rachel sighed. "It's not fair—I wish you could keep her. She loves you!"

Anna giggled. "Only because I feed her a ton of food, and she's so hungry. I think she looks bigger already, and we've only had her a day."

"It isn't just that. She looks so happy. And beautiful, now that you've brushed her and she has a new collar and leash."

Anna had spent most of her vacation money at the vet, buying things for Sandy. But she didn't mind. Even if Sandy did go to the shelter, she was much more likely to be adopted if she was well groomed and had a nice collar on, wasn't she? Anna hated the thought of Sandy being stuck at the shelter, with nobody to pet her and pay attention to her and love her. *Like I would,* she added silently.

Rachel's mom was just coming along the waterfront path as they got to Anna's beach house. They waved to her.

"Thanks for inviting us on the picnic,"

Anna said. "I'll just stop in and ask Mom and Dad, okay? Oh, no...." She made a face. "I can hear Jeannie crying—she's teething."

Dad came to let her in. "Sorry about the noise," he said to Rachel's mom with a frazzled sort of smile. "Poor Jeannie. She's really miserable. Anna's mom is upstairs catching up on some sleep."

Rachel's mom started to explain about the picnic, and Anna and Rachel went over to see Jeannie. She was in her car seat—it looked like Dad had been rocking her. Her cheeks were red, and she was making sad little hiccupping noises.

"Hello, Jeannie," Anna crooned. "Are your teeth still hurting? Poor baby...." And she rocked the car seat gently.

Rachel and Sandy watched, but the rocking didn't seem to help—Jeannie's crying only got louder.

"It's okay, Sandy," Rachel whispered, seeing the dog's ears twitching worriedly. "I don't think Sandy likes the noise."

Anna looked around, wondering if she should move Sandy away from Jeannie, but the little dog crept forward and laid her nose very gently on the car seat. She gave a quiet whine and stared at Jeannie.

Jeannie stopped crying at once and stared back, looking surprised—at least, Anna thought she did. It was hard to tell with babies sometimes. She gazed into Sandy's dark eyes and made a sort of cooing sound.

Dad looked down at Jeannie and

smiled. "That's the first time she's stopped crying all afternoon!" he said. "Good girl, Sandy. She's been very good around Jeannie, actually," he explained to Rachel's mom. "I was worried about having a dog with a baby, but maybe if we're very careful…."

Anna and Rachel exchanged a delighted look. Sandy was definitely winning Dad over!

"Mom and Dad are still making sandwiches, so they sent us to get you," Zach explained.

"Okay, I'll go and tell Mom and Dad you're here. I don't think they're quite ready. Can you put Sandy's leash on, Rachel?" Anna handed Rachel the leash, and Sandy wriggled and yapped, trying to catch it in her teeth. She loved walks.

Dad came down the stairs and laughed at Sandy jumping around. "Poor Sandy—you can't make her wait now, Anna. She might fall over from the excitement. Why don't the two of you walk over with Zach and Rachel, and we'll catch up to you in a minute?"

Rachel went to hand the leash back to Anna when they got out the front door, but Anna shook her head. "You can hold her if you want to," she told Rachel. She knew how much Rachel would love a dog, even though she adored Barney, their little orange cat. She'd shown Anna pictures of him. He had the brightest pink nose Anna had ever seen on a cat.

They walked to Rachel and Zach's house along the waterfront path, past many other people with dogs and children who stopped to pet her. Anna watched Sandy proudly—she looked so pretty, and she was walking nicely for Rachel, too.

Sandy trotted along, sniffing happily at all the good smells along the bottom of the railings and enjoying the attention that the children were giving her. It was so nice to be patted and told she was a good dog.

She glanced up at Anna to check that she was still there and hadn't disappeared, and then looked ahead to see where they were going. She stopped short with a frightened whimper. She knew that dog. That big, fierce, yellow dog, who was coming toward them.

He'd spotted her, too, and he growled loudly, pulling hard on his leash. The dog was going to chase her again!

Sandy whimpered and darted backward, nearly tripping Rachel up. Zach and Anna both made a grab for her leash to help, but Sandy yanked it out of Rachel's hand and shot across the road, desperate to get away from the big Labrador.

A car braked suddenly and the driver started to yell at the three children,

but they were already darting across the
road behind him, racing after Sandy.

Chapter Eight
Welcome to the Family

"I'm really sorry!" Rachel gasped. "I didn't mean to let go—she pulled so hard!"

"It wasn't your fault," Anna panted back. "She was really scared of that Labrador. I don't know why. She didn't mind any of the other dogs."

"We're really close to our house," Zach said. "She did go down here, didn't she? I bet she's on the grass somewhere."

Anna nodded. There was a cold feeling in her stomach, and she was trying hard not to cry. Just when Dad had started to think about keeping Sandy! She'd heard him talking to Mom about it the night before—about how good Sandy was and how responsible Anna was being, trying to take care of the puppy and find her owners. They wouldn't think Anna was responsible now that Sandy had gotten lost again!

"We'll find her," Zach said. "Don't worry. Come on."

They raced across the little lawn, looking and calling.

"At least she has her leash on," Anna said, her voice wobbling. "If anyone sees her, they'll know she's slipped away. They might even be able to grab the leash."

"Should I get Mom and Dad and Lily to come and look, too?" Zach suggested.

"No, I'm sure she went running over the lawn," Rachel said. "If we stop and get Mom and Dad, she might go somewhere else. We need to find her now!"

Anna nodded. Rachel was right. "Sandy!" she called, her voice squeaky with fright. "Sandy, come on! Come on, sweetheart!" Then she gave a little gasp. "Oh! The dog treats—I brought a packet with me to be her part of the picnic. I got them at the vet for her." She rummaged in her pocket and pulled out the foil packet. Then she shook it gently so that the treats rattled around inside. "Here, Sandy! Yummy treats, come on!"

She shook them again, but Sandy didn't come. "I was sure she'd want them...." Anna whispered. "I don't think she's here. She must have run down to the next street."

"No! Look, I can see her!" Rachel grabbed Anna's arm. "Isn't that her, over in that yard? I'm sure I saw something move when you shook the treats."

Anna looked over and saw a pale shape curled up under a bush. "It is her!" she whispered. "Oh, you're the best, Rachel. Don't run!" she added to Zach, who looked as though he was about to dash into the yard. "She's really scared. She might race off again."

"Okay." Zach nodded. "You creep up and call her."

"Sandy...," Anna called gently. "Sandy, come here, sweetheart." She gave the bag of treats another shake.

Sandy looked up, a little golden face surrounded by pink and purple flowers. She looked beautiful—except that she was trembling.

"It's all right," Anna called, standing by the wall. "Come on." She patted her knees gently and Sandy crept a touch closer. But she didn't get up and run to Anna.

Anna glanced at the house and hoped the owners wouldn't mind if she went into their yard. She walked onto the path and bent down. "Come on, Sandy...."

This time, Sandy wriggled out from under the bush. She crept over to Anna, her head down, still shaking.

"Poor Sandy," Anna said, as she gripped the leash tightly and rubbed Sandy's trembling ears. "That big dog really scared you, didn't he?"

Suddenly, Sandy jerked on her leash again, and Anna glanced around. The front door was opening—and a familiar-looking elderly lady glared at her.

"Oh, no," Anna breathed. It was the same lady she'd woken up a couple of days before. "I'm sorry," she said out loud. "I didn't mean to disturb you. Sandy got scared by another dog and ran away and then she hid under your flowers. We're just leaving." She could see Mom and Dad coming up the street now, with Jeannie in her stroller. She really hoped they weren't going to be angry.

The elderly lady frowned. "But wasn't it you who came to the door a couple of days ago?"

"Yes," Anna admitted, feeling glad that Rachel and Zach had come over to stand by the wall now.

"Anna thought Sandy was ours," Rachel explained. "But she isn't. No one knows who she belongs to, but Anna's taking care of her. It was my fault she's in your yard. I let go of her leash." She looked over apologetically at Anna's mom and dad, who had arrived at the house. "I'm sorry. I should have held her tighter."

"But you're all okay?" Anna's dad asked worriedly. "We only saw that you were trying to call Sandy out of the yard."

"We're fine," Anna said. "Sandy got scared by a big dog. I think she might have met him before. It was like she knew him, and he really frightened her."

"I saw your posters," the elderly lady broke in suddenly. "I didn't realize it was the same dog. I have seen her before, you know, now that I see her up close."

"Have you?" Anna gulped, wondering if the lady knew who Sandy's owners were. She crouched down and put her arms around the little dog. What if she was about to lose Sandy again?

"On the beach. Yes, I'm sure it was her. Two or three times over the summer and never with the same people."

"So she's definitely a stray?" Anna's mom said slowly, looking over at her dad.

The lady nodded. "Poor little thing. I don't think she can belong to anyone."

Mom smiled at Anna. "I don't think that's true, Anna, do you?"

Anna took a deep breath of relief and smiled shakily back at her mom. Then

she buried her nose in Sandy's frizzy ears. Sandy nuzzled her damp nose against Anna's cheek.

Then she looked up at the elderly lady and shook her head. "She does," she explained. "Now she belongs to me."

Anna curled up on the chair in front of Mom's computer and carefully typed Rachel's email address. Mom had written it down in her address book so she wouldn't lose it.

> To: Rachel
> From: Anna
> Subject: Sandy!

Hi Rachel!

I can't believe summer vacation is almost over! Do you go back to school next week, like we do?

Mom and I took Sandy to the vet yesterday, and the vet said she was beautiful. He said Sandy was probably a mixture of a poodle and something else—that's why she's so curly! The vet said we have to be very careful with Sandy's thick fur—we're going to have to take her to get groomed at a special dog salon!

She has a microchip now, so even if she gets lost again, we'll get her back. And we went to get a tag for her collar with Mom and Dad's numbers on it, too! This is a photo of Sandy with her tag on. I feel like she's really ours now!

Lots of love from Sandy and me—and Sandy says hi to Barney.

Anna xxx

Anna pressed send and looked down at Sandy, who was curled up under the desk, waiting for her to finish. Sandy looked so beautiful now, with her coat clean and brushed. She was definitely less skinny, too.

Sandy jumped up, putting her front paws on Anna's knees, her fluffy golden tail wagging. Then she rested her chin on Anna's lap and stared up at her adoringly.

"It was the best vacation ever," Anna whispered to her, petting Sandy's curly ears. "But it's so nice to be home—especially now that it's your home, too."

HOLLY WEBB

Holly Webb started out as a children's book editor, and wrote her first series for the publisher she worked for. She has been writing ever since, with more than 100 books to her name. Holly lives in England with her husband, three young sons, and several cats who are always nosing around when she is trying to type on her laptop.

For more information
about Holly Webb visit:

www.holly-webb.com
www.tigertalesbooks.com